PUFFIN BOOKS

Not Quite a Mermaid
MERMAID SURPRISE

Linda Chapman lives in Leicestershire with
her family and two Bernese mountain dogs.
When she is not writing she spends her time
looking after her two young daughters,
horse riding and teaching drama.

Books by Linda Chapman

MY SECRET UNICORN Series
NOT QUITE A MERMAID Series
STARDUST Series

BRIGHT LIGHTS
CENTRE STAGE

Not Quite a Mermaid

MERMAID SURPRISE

LINDA CHAPMAN

Illustrated by Dawn Apperley

PUFFIN

PUFFIN BOOKS

Published by the Penguin Group
Penguin Books Ltd, 80 Strand, London WC2R 0RL, England
Penguin Group (USA) Inc., 375 Hudson Street, New York, New York 10014, USA
Penguin Group (Canada), 90 Eglinton Avenue East, Suite 700, Toronto, Ontario,
Canada M4P 2Y3 (a division of Pearson Penguin Canada Inc.)
Penguin Ireland, 25 St Stephen's Green, Dublin 2, Ireland
(a division of Penguin Books Ltd)
Penguin Group (Australia), 250 Camberwell Road, Camberwell, Victoria 3124, Australia
(a division of Pearson Australia Group Pty Ltd)
Penguin Books India Pvt Ltd, 11 Community Centre, Panchsheel Park,
New Delhi – 110 017, India
Penguin Group (NZ), 67 Apollo Drive, Rosedale, North Shore 0632, New Zealand
(a division of Pearson New Zealand Ltd)
Penguin Books (South Africa) (Pty) Ltd, 24 Sturdee Avenue, Rosebank,
Johannesburg 2196, South Africa

Penguin Books Ltd, Registered Offices: 80 Strand, London WC2R 0RL, England

puffinbooks.com

Published 2007
1

Text copyright © Linda Chapman, 2007
Illustrations copyright © Dawn Apperley, 2007
All rights reserved

The moral right of the author and illustrator has been asserted

Set in Palatino 15/27 pt
Typeset by Palimpsest Book Production Limited, Grangemouth, Stirlingshire
Made and printed in England by Clays Ltd, St Ives plc

British Library Cataloguing in Publication Data
A CIP catalogue record for this book is available from the British Library

ISBN: 978–0–141–32229–2

lindachapman.co.uk

To db, who told me about sea mice . . .

Contents

Chapter One

'A giant sea snake!' exclaimed Electra, the mermaid. She stared at her mum.

'Yes,' Maris replied, her green eyes serious. 'It's been seen swimming outside the reef wall. It's only a baby. It shouldn't be able to get through the wall but there's just a chance it might wriggle through a crack and get into the caves.'

'Wow!' Electra looked at Splash, the young dolphin who was swimming nearby. 'Did you hear that, Splash? Shall we go and see if we can find it?'

'OK!' Splash whistled. He lived with Maris and Electra because his own parents had been killed by sharks. He and Electra were best friends. 'I've

never seen a giant sea snake before,'
he said.

'Me neither!' Electra spun round in
the water in excitement, her long red
hair swirling around her. 'It'll be an
adventure!'

'Electra! Splash!' Maris said as if
she couldn't believe her ears. 'You are
not going to see the sea snake! Giant
sea snakes are very dangerous. Even
though a baby one can't eat you, it
could still give you a nasty bite. I will
not allow you to go and see it!'

'But, Mum, it's only a baby . . .'
Electra began.

'No, Electra.' Maris put her hands on her hips and swished her tail.

Electra could tell from the strict look on her mum's face that there was no point in arguing. Maris, like all the other merpeople who lived in the warm shallow waters around Mermaid Island, didn't like doing adventurous things. They liked staying inside the coral reef that surrounded Mermaid Island like a circular wall. But Electra was different. She loved having exciting adventures! Luckily Splash did too.

'I've got to go out to the shops now,' Maris went on. 'I've asked Ronan if

you two can go
and play with Sam
and Sasha for the
afternoon.'

Sam and Sasha and
their dad, Ronan, lived
in the next-door cave.
Sam and Sasha were
twins. They were almost a
year younger than Electra,
and she and Splash were very good
friends with them.

'OK.' Electra would rather have gone
out looking for a baby sea snake but
playing with the twins would be fun.

'And try not to get into trouble while you're there,' Maris said.

'We won't,' Electra replied. 'Will we, Splash?'

'Of course not!' Splash said, staring at Maris with bright, innocent eyes.

'Hmmm,' Maris said, not looking so sure.

Maris, Electra and Splash swam next door. Electra put her mermaid bag over her shoulder, hung on to Splash's fin and kicked with her feet. Liking adventures wasn't the *only* thing that made her different from the other merpeople. While they all had tails, she had legs and feet. This was because Electra had been born a human.

She had been washed up near Mermaid Island in a small boat after a dreadful storm one night eight years ago. She had just been a baby at the time. The merpeople had found Electra and decided to bring her up as a mermaid. They had given her magic sea powder so she could breathe underwater and then Maris, a young mermaid, who had no other children, had adopted her. Now, Electra couldn't imagine being anything but a mermaid.

'Hi!' Sam and Sasha came to the cave doorway to meet them when Maris rang the conch-shell bell. The twins both had very blonde hair. Sam's was short. Sasha's reached her shoulders and she usually put a plait in it on one side.

'Come in,' Sam said.

'I'll be back to collect you at tea time,' Maris told Electra and Splash. She kissed them both. 'Be good.'

'Bye, Mum,' Electra called as Maris swam away.

'Dad's inside – and so's Gran,' Sam told Electra and Splash.

Electra was pleased. She really liked the twins' grandmother. Some of the older merpeople gave Electra strange looks because she didn't have a tail, but the twins' gran was always really nice to her. If she ever brought Sam and Sasha any sweets she always made sure she brought a big bag for Electra and Splash too.

'It's Gran's birthday today,' Sasha told Electra as they swam through the shell curtain that hung in the cave doorway. Inside was a round table made of mother-of-pearl, a big sofa and three comfy chairs made from large blue basket sponges, and squashy cushions made out of smaller lilac sponges. A purple seaweed rug covered the floor. Everywhere was very neat and tidy – but then it always was. Ronan hated mess.

The twins' gran was sitting on one of the comfy chairs. She was an old mermaid with long grey hair, a lined face and green eyes that twinkled. 'Hello, dear,' she said, smiling at

Electra. 'The twins told me you were coming round and luckily . . .' she paused to rummage in the mermaid bag she had beside her, '. . . I had brought these for you and Splash.'

She handed Electra a bag crammed full of tiny rainbow-coloured sugar starfish.

'Thank you,' Electra said in delight – sugar starfish were her favourite sweets. She put the sweets into her bag and gave Gran a hug. 'I should be giving you a present, though. Sasha says it's your birthday.'

'Don't worry about that, dear,' Gran said kindly. 'When you get to my age you don't mind about birthdays.'

Electra was shocked. 'I'll *always* mind about birthdays! Aren't you having a cake and a party?'

'Oh, no, no,' Gran said, shaking her head. 'That sort of thing is for young people. My party days are over.' She looked sad for a moment. 'I did have some good times when I was just a young mermaid – and some lovely presents. Do you know what the best present I ever had was?' she said to Electra and the others.

'A new bikini?' Sasha suggested.

'A horn made out of a conch shell?' asked Sam.

'A trip somewhere really exciting?' said Electra.

'No.' Gran smiled. 'It was a sea mouse.'

'A sea mouse!' Electra echoed. Sea mice were small furry fish with tails and little round ears that lived in the deeper waters of the reef.

'Yes.' Gran's eyes hazed over as

she remembered. 'My grandmother bought him for me. I called him Sandy because he had a sandy-coloured coat. He was so sweet. He used to swim up and sit on my shoulder and nuzzle my face with his little nose. He was my pet – and my best friend. I cried so much when he got old and died.' She looked wistful. 'He really was the best present I ever had.'

Just then, Ronan came in from the kitchen. 'Hello, Electra,' he said cheerfully. 'Hi, Splash!'

'Hi, Ronan!' Electra and Splash chorused.

Ronan swam over to Gran. 'Are you ready to go out?'

Gran nodded and with a flick of her tail she swam up from the chair.

'See you later,' Ronan said to Electra and the others. 'Gran and I are going to see some of her friends. We'll be back by tea time. Have fun until then but don't make a mess.' He watched as Gran swam to the cave entrance and then lowered his voice. 'Remember the cards,' he whispered to Sam and Sasha.

They nodded. 'We will!' Sam said with a grin.

'See you later!' Gran called and she and Ronan swam out through the shell curtain.

'The cards?' Electra said to Sam and Sasha.

'We're going to make some birthday cards for Gran,' explained Sam.

'Can I do one too?' Electra asked eagerly.

'Of course. And Splash can help,'
Sasha said, giving Splash a stroke.

Sam and Sasha fetched some pens
and they all started to draw out some

cards. Electra drew a picture of a sea mouse on hers and wrote 'Happy Birthday!' in big purple letters.

She coloured it in, but after five minutes she had finished and began to feel bored. Sam and Sasha were colouring in very slowly. Splash had given up trying to draw with his mouth and was amusing himself by seeing how many pens he could balance on his nose. He looked rather bored too.

What else can we do? Electra thought. *We can't do this all afternoon.* She looked around the tidy cave. What could they do that would be fun?

Sam was carefully colouring in a birthday cake on his card. 'It must feel weird to be old and not have a proper birthday with presents and a party and things,' he said.

'Yes,' Sasha agreed. 'I'll never get too old for parties.'

An idea popped into Electra's head. 'That's it!' she gasped. 'That's what we can do!'

The others looked at her.

'What do you mean?' Sam said, puzzled.

'This afternoon!' Electra said. 'I've been trying to think of something fun that we can do and now I know!' A wide grin spread across her face. 'We can organize a surprise birthday party for your gran!'

Chapter Two

Electra looked round at the others. 'Well, what do you think?'

'Oh, yes!' Sasha exclaimed, clasping her hands together in delight. 'We can make a birthday banner.'

'And streamers!' cried Sam.

'And a cake!' said Electra eagerly.

'We don't know how to make a cake,' Sasha said doubtfully.

'Dad never lets us because he says we'd make too much mess,' Sam put in.

'I bet I can make a cake!' Electra

said, waving a hand airily. 'I've seen my mum do it *loads* of times.'

'We'll give Gran the best birthday surprise ever!' Splash said in excitement.

Electra grinned. 'Why don't Splash and I do the cake?' she said, looking at the twins. 'While you two do the banners and streamers.'

Sam and Sasha nodded and swam over to one of the cupboards to get some paints and paper out to make a banner and streamers.

Meanwhile, Electra and Splash headed to the kitchen.

'We need mermaid flour, eggs,

sugar and butter,' Electra said, trying to remember what her mum used. She opened all the cupboards and found the one with cake ingredients in. As she began to pull things out, she saw a large packet of chocolate chips. 'Oh, and we need these,' she said. 'These will be very good in a cake!'

'What do we do next?' Splash asked eagerly when Electra had found all the ingredients, a mixing bowl and an enormous cake tin.

Electra hesitated. She wasn't actually too sure. She sometimes stirred the cake mixture when her mum was

making cakes – and she liked licking the bowl afterwards – but she'd never really taken much notice of what her mum had been doing. But then how difficult could it be to make a cake?

'It's easy! You just put everything in a bowl and stir it round,' she said.

'Then you put it all into the oven with some mermaid fire to cook it.' She began to open the packets of ingredients. The chocolate chips smelt delicious.

Splash nosed the bag. 'Maybe we should taste these – just to check they haven't gone off,' he suggested.

Electra grinned. 'OK.'

They each ate a chocolate chip. 'They taste all right to me,' Splash said.

'Maybe we should just try a few more to be on the safe side,' Electra said.

They ate some more – and then some more.

Five minutes later the bag was empty.

Splash whistled happily. 'I like cooking!' he said.

'Me too!' Electra gave a chocolatey grin. Picking up the bag of flour, she emptied it all into the bowl. Then she threw in the butter and sugar and cracked the eggs open and emptied them in too. She wasn't sure how many eggs to use so she used them all. Then she began to stir. It was hard work. The ingredients just didn't seem to want to stay in the bowl. A blob landed on the table, then another went on the floor and then another landed with a splat on Splash's tail.

He laughed. 'Let me have a go!'

He took the spoon in his mouth and whizzed round in a circle. The cake mix flew everywhere.

'Stop, Splash!' Electra giggled, ducking as some cake mix flew at her head.

Splash stopped and looked into the bowl. 'At least it's all mixed up,' he said.

Electra nodded and tipped the gloopy mess into the cake tin. 'There we are.' She patted the mixture down. 'Now, we just need to put it in the oven.' She carried the tin over to the oven. She knew that to make a

mermaid oven
work you had
to put in some
mermaid
fire.
Ronan, like
all merpeople,
kept some
mermaid fire in

a large container beside the oven. But how much should she use? Electra didn't have a clue. Guessing wildly, she reached in and took a large ball of glowing green mermaid fire out of the pot. 'This'll do!'

'That looks quite a lot,' Splash said doubtfully.

'It'll be fine,' said Electra, sticking the fire inside the oven. 'Come on. Let's go and see how the twins are doing with the banner and the streamers!'

The twins had made a big banner on which they had painted the words 'HAPPY BIRTHDAY GRAN!' They had hung it on one wall and were in the middle of making lots of streamers.

'Oh, wow! The banner looks great!' Electra said.

'Come and help us with these,' Sam said, pointing to the streamers.

They had great fun shaking glitter on to the streamers then hanging them up from rocky hooks on the cave walls. By the time they had finished they all had glitter in their hair.

'It looks wonderful!' Electra said happily.

Sam frowned. 'Everywhere is very messy, though.'

'Dad's not going to like it,' Sasha said, looking round at the paint and glitter on the floor and all the open paint pots and dirty brushes.

'We'll clear up later,' Electra said airily. 'Right now we need to think about presents! What shall we . . .' She broke off as a smoky smell hit the back of her throat. 'What's that smell? Oh, no!' she gasped as she realized what it must be. 'It's the cake! It must be burning!'

Chapter Three

Electra raced to the kitchen with the others following. Black smoke was billowing out of the oven.

'Oh!' Electra said, opening the oven door.

The cake had grown, puffing up

over the sides of the tin. It had also turned black.

'It's burnt!' Sasha exclaimed.

Electra grabbed some oven gloves and took the cake out of the oven. 'It's not that bad,' she said as she put it down on the table. 'We can just cut the burnt bits off. I'm sure it'll taste OK.' She prodded it with a finger. It was as

hard as a rock. 'I . . . um . . . I think,' she added doubtfully.

'We can't give Gran a burnt cake,' Sam said in dismay.

Electra's eyes fell on some tubes of icing sugar in the open cupboard. 'I know!' she exclaimed. 'Leave it to me! Why don't you go and finish the birthday cards and I'll sort the cake out.'

'Are you sure you can?' Sasha said dubiously.

Electra nodded.

'OK then,' Sam said, and he and Sasha swam off.

'What are you going to do?' Splash asked Electra curiously.

'This.'

Electra picked off the burnt bits on top of the cake. Luckily the cake seemed a bit softer right in the middle. She picked off the burnt bits on the sides too. By the time she had got rid of all the burnt bits the cake was very small – only big enough for one person – and it was a bit lopsided. *Maybe it will look better with icing*, Electra thought hopefully.

She iced the cake pink and finished by writing 'Happy Birthday' in swirly letters on the top. 'There!' she said. 'It looks much better!'

'I guess,' Splash said, not sounding convinced.

'Well, it will have to do!' Electra

quickly swept the burnt remains of the cake into her bag so that no one would see them. 'Come on, let's go and get the others. We've got to get a present sorted out.'

Sam and Sasha were just finishing their cards.

'We need to think about a present for Gran. What shall we get her?' Electra asked.

'A box of chocolates,' Sam suggested.

'But we haven't got any money,' Sasha pointed out. 'Why don't we get some anemones and put them in a pot for her?'

'I guess,' Electra said doubtfully. It sounded a rather boring present.

'Or we could make a shell necklace for her,' Sasha suggested.

'There must be something more exciting we can get her than that.' Electra stroked Splash. 'If only we knew what she really wanted.'

'I know!' Splash whistled suddenly. 'A sea mouse!'

Electra stared at him. 'Of course!' she cried. 'Gran said that a sea mouse was the best present she'd ever had and we can get one for free if we go to the deep caves and find one!'

'We can't go to the deep caves!' protested Sasha.

'No! It's much too dangerous. There might be a giant sea snake there!' Sam exclaimed.

'We'll be very quick,' Electra said.

'And it'll be an adventure,' said Splash.

'We could just whizz to the caves, get a sea mouse and whizz back,' Electra said. 'And even if the snake has got into the caves, well, it's only a baby one.'

The twins looked very doubtful.

'We'd be doing it for Gran,' Electra told them persuasively. 'Think how happy she would be. I bet a sea mouse is the only thing she's wanted for years

and years and no one has ever got her one. Poor Gran.' She looked at Sam's and Sasha's uncertain faces. 'I bet if we got her one, she wouldn't stop smiling for . . . for a whole *year*!'

'I suppose it would make her happy,' Sam said, looking tempted.

'Sam!' Sasha exclaimed. 'We can't go!'

Electra saw that Sam was weakening. 'Just think of Gran, all happy and smiling,' she said to him. 'And if we do see the sea snake, well, it's only a tiny, baby one and we'll easily be able to swim away from it . . .'

'All right. I'll come!' Sam decided.

He swam to the entrance and joined Electra and Splash.

'Wait! What about me?' Sasha wailed. 'I don't want to be left here on my own!'

'Come with us then,' urged Electra.

'Yes, go on, Sasha!' Splash said. 'Pleeeeease!'

'Oh, all right!' Sasha said. 'But we just go there and back,' she added quickly to Electra. 'No exploring. No trying to see the sea snake. No . . .'

But Electra wasn't listening. 'Come on!' she cried, diving out through the shell curtain. 'Let's go!'

Chapter Four

Electra and the others swam down through the turquoise water. Shoals of stripy orange clownfish and silvery angelfish swooshed around them. Electra twirled around in the glowing cloud of fish. Excitement was buzzing through her. This was going to be fun!

As they got closer to the deepest caves, they saw huge clams with open mouths. White and pink anemones covered the rocks, their fronds waving in the water. The water changed from turquoise to indigo. Electra knew it never got really dark in the waters around Mermaid Island. It was

different, though, out in the deep sea beyond the reef. There the water got as black as the night sky. Electra had swum out there a few times and had seen all sorts of weird fish with sharp fangs, gulper eels and hungry sharks.

The deepest caves in the reef around Mermaid Island were usually safe, although sometimes dangerous creatures like the giant sea snake did manage to find their way in.

But it's just a baby sea snake, Electra told herself. *It won't be able to hurt us much and we'll probably be able to swim away from it. I bet we won't see it anyway.*

They reached the entrance to the caves. A rocky barrier had been put up by the adult merpeople to keep the snake out of the waters on the inside of the reef in case it did find its way through the caves and tunnels. It didn't take Electra long to pull out enough rocks so that there was a hole big enough for them all to swim through.

'We must be quick,' said Sasha. 'What if Dad comes back early and finds we're not at home?'

'We won't be long,' Electra reassured her. 'We'll just swim to the first cave, scoop up a sea mouse and take it home. Come on!'

They swam through the hole and into the tunnel that linked the caves. It was quite dark and Electra swam to the bottom of the tunnel and, touching it, said, *'From the deeps of the sea, mermaid fire come to me!'*

A stream of glowing green mermaid fire flooded into her hands and formed into a ball. Electra placed some of it in the tunnel so that they could see. As they swam along she put a ball of fire down every so often so that they could see through the gloom. However, to Electra's surprise, there wasn't actually much to see at all.

In the first cave they came to, although there were spiny sea urchins and a carpet of pale anemones, there were no sea mice. The sea mice could usually be seen swimming along the bottom of the sea, their bright eyes darting from side to side, their coats fluffing up in the water. But today there wasn't a single one.

'Where have all the sea mice gone?' Splash said in surprise.

'I don't know.' Electra glanced around. 'There are no other fish either.'

'And no sea horses or crabs,' Sam pointed out.

Electra frowned. Usually there were lots of fish and small creatures in the caves. 'I wonder where they have all gone?'

'Maybe they're further in,' Splash suggested.

They swam further along the tunnels but every cave they came to was completely empty.

'I don't like this,' Sasha said, looking worried. 'It's like the fish and other creatures are hiding from something.'

Electra's skin began to prickle. Sasha was right. Something didn't feel quite normal.

'I think we should go back,' Sasha said nervously.

Electra hesitated. She *really* wanted to get a sea mouse for Gran. 'Let's just go on to one more cave . . .'

Sasha interrupted her with a squeal. 'Electra! Look!'

Electra swung round and gasped. A black and red sea snake was swimming round the bend in the tunnel ahead. It was about as long as Electra's arm from her elbow to her hand.

Sam yelled.

'Quick!' Sasha cried, panicking. 'Come on!'

'Wait!' Electra exclaimed. 'Look how small it is! We don't need to run away from that.'

Sam and Sasha paused in mid flight. 'I guess it is really small,' Sam said hesitantly.

'I'm not scared of it,' Electra declared.

'Me neither,' Splash said bravely. But then he gave an alarmed whistle as another sea snake came wriggling round the corner – and *this* one was

massive, at least as long as three grown-up mermaids. It had a nasty, hungry look in its beady black eyes. 'I *am* scared of that, though!' he exclaimed.

'It must be the baby's mum!' Electra gasped. 'Swim, everyone!'

The mother sea snake suddenly caught sight of them. Eyes gleaming hungrily, she swam straight towards them!

Chapter Five

Yelling in alarm, Electra and the others turned round and began to swim as fast as they could. Electra grabbed Splash's fin. She kicked hard, her heart pounding as he plunged through the water. The mother sea snake was huge and judging by her skinny body she was very hungry too!

'This must be why the caves were empty,' Electra gasped to Splash. 'All the fish must be hiding from the sea snakes!'

'I wish I was hiding too!' Splash said, swerving through the water as fast as he could go.

Luckily, although sea snakes could swim very quickly, mermaids and dolphins were even quicker.

Electra glanced behind her. The mother sea snake seemed to be giving up. She was definitely slowing down. 'Phew!' Electra called. 'I think she's given up chasing us.'

'Thank goodness!' Sasha exclaimed.

The mother sea snake stopped.

'I just want to get out of here,' said Sam.

They were passing a cave. Electra glanced inside. A sea mouse was swimming around inside it, its pointed

nose nudging along the floor, its bright eyes looking round the cave. 'Wait, Splash!' Electra exclaimed, remembering why they had come to the caves in the first place. 'Look! There's a sea mouse. Let's see if it wants to come with us.'

'What about the snake?' Splash demanded.

'It's given up. It's not chasing us

any more,' Electra said. 'It'll only take a second to get the mouse.'

Splash dived into the cave.

'What are you doing?' Sam shouted after them.

'Getting a sea mouse. We'll catch up with you in a minute!' Electra called.

Letting go of Splash's fin, she swam to the floor of the cave and crouched down

in front of the sea mouse. It looked at her inquisitively. 'Hello, I'm Electra,' she told it. 'Would you like to come with us and be Gran's new pet? I know she'll look after you really well and she'll love you very much. She really likes sea mice.'

The sea mouse hesitated. Its whiskers twitched.

'Isn't it cute?' Electra said to Splash.

'Yes,' Splash agreed. 'But we should go soon.'

Just then the mouse looked towards the cave entrance, gave a terrified squeak and shot out of Electra's hands and into a nearby patch of anemones. Electra swung round. Her heart missed a beat. 'Splash! Look!'

The mother and the baby sea snake were wriggling in the entrance to the cave. The mother hadn't given up at all! She'd just been waiting for the baby to catch up with her!

'What do we do?' Electra gasped to Splash.

'I don't know,' he replied.

The mother sea snake opened her mouth and gave a wicked hiss. She and her baby started to swim into the cave.

'Help!' Splash cried. He and Electra swam back until they reached the cave wall and stopped. There was no escape! They were trapped!

'Electra! Splash!'

It was Sam and Sasha. They had swum back to the cave entrance. They stared in horror at the two hissing snakes wriggling towards Electra and Splash.

'Get back!' Electra shouted

to them. 'Swim away before the snakes see you!'

But it was too late. The mother snake swung round and saw the twins.

Sam and Sasha hesitated and, for a moment, Electra thought they were going to do the sensible thing and swim away but then Sam dived forward. 'Go away!' he shouted bravely to the snakes. 'Leave our friends alone!'

Looking terrified, Sasha joined him. 'You're horrid!' she exclaimed. Electra could hear her voice shaking. 'Horrid, horrid, horrid!'

The snake's eyes gleamed and she

shot through the water towards Sam and Sasha. Sam dived out of the way but, to Electra's horror, Sasha just seemed to freeze with fear.

'Swim, Sasha!' Electra yelled.

But Sasha didn't move. Her mouth opened and shut. Her green eyes were wide with terror. The snake reared up in front of her and opened its mouth.

Electra couldn't bear it any longer. 'No!' she shrieked. She looked around desperately for a weapon but the only thing she had was her mermaid bag. It would have to do! She hoisted it up to bash the snake with. It was very heavy. *The burnt cake bits!* Electra realized.

She had an idea. Opening her bag, she grabbed one of the burnt pieces of cake. She threw it as hard as she could at the mother snake.

The cake bounced off the snake's back. The snake swung round.

Electra threw another piece of cake. This time the snake instinctively opened her jaws. She snapped the cake up and bit hard.

'She's eating it!' Splash exclaimed.

Electra chucked another piece of cake. The snake gobbled it up so fast she didn't even seem to taste it.

'I think she likes it!' Splash said.

Electra began to throw all the remaining pieces out of the bag. They fell through the water like stones. Both snakes chased the pieces through the water, snapping them up in quick bites.

'Quick!' Electra said to Splash. 'Let's escape while they're busy eating.'

They plunged over the snakes' heads and raced to the entrance.

'Come on!' Sam cried.

Electra glanced over her shoulder. The snakes' skinny bodies were full of lumps now, where the cake they had gobbled up had stuck. The mother snake hesitated by the last piece of cake and then looked round at the lump in its tummy. She swayed suddenly and shut her eyes. The baby snake flopped to the ground.

'They don't look very well!' said Splash.

The snakes' scales began to turn a greenish colour and their tummies bulged even more. The mother snake opened her mouth and gave a weak hiss. Her tummy rumbled like a volcano.

A grin caught at the corner of Electra's mouth. She reached in her bag. There was just one piece of cake left. She threw it towards the mother snake. 'Here, Snaky, have some cake!' The snake looked at the cake in horror and then turned and raced out of the cave. The baby followed her.

'They've gone!' Sasha exclaimed.

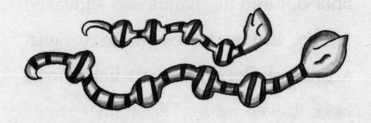

'Hooray!' Sam shouted.

They all hugged each other then Electra swam to the patch of anemones where the sea mouse was hiding. All she could see was its little nose and twitching whiskers. She held out her hands and spoke softly. 'Are you coming with us, little sea mouse? If you do, you'll never have to worry about sea snakes again!'

The sea mouse didn't hesitate. It shot out into her hands and squeaked loudly. Electra kissed its furry head. 'Come on, let's take you home,' she said.

Chapter Six

Electra and the others swam quickly out of the hole Electra had made in the barrier. They filled it in just in case the snakes decided to come back and then raced back home to the twins' cave.

'Phew!' Sam said as they dived in

through the curtain and realized that the cave was empty. 'Dad and Gran aren't back yet!'

'Luckily,' Electra said, looking around at the mess. The painting and decorating things they had used were still out, the floor was covered with glitter, the banner was dripping paint on to the rug, and the streamers had half fallen down. And then there was the kitchen . . .

What was Ronan going to say when he saw all the mess?

'I think we'd better clean up,' she said hastily.

But just then, the shell curtain tinkled behind them.

'We're back!' Ronan called, swimming into the cave with Gran. 'Have you been good and . . .' He broke off and stared in shock at the cave. 'What's happened here?' he gasped.

Electra's heart sank. Oh, no, now they were in trouble!

'Look at the mess!' Ronan exclaimed angrily. 'What's been going on?'

Sam and Sasha looked at the floor. Splash didn't say anything. Electra felt awful. 'We . . . er . . . we just wanted to have a surprise party for Gran,' she stammered. 'We were going to tidy up. We'll do it now.'

'Yes, you will,' Ronan said crossly as Gran swam past him into the cave. 'This is . . .'

'Beautiful,' Gran interrupted him. She clasped her hands and looked around the cave at the wonky streamers and the painted banner. 'Happy Birthday, Gran,' she read out. 'Oh, my dears,' she said, swimming over and gathering Sam and Sasha into a huge hug. 'I love it!' She smiled at Electra. 'And I think I know whose idea it was.'

'It was mine,' Electra admitted.

Gran smiled at her. 'Thank you.'

'We've also got a present for you,' Electra said, swimming over to her. 'I hope you like it.' She took the sea mouse out of her bag.

'A sea mouse!' Gran exclaimed.

The mouse sat up on Electra's hand and looked around, his whiskers twitching and his eyes bright.

'It's for you,' Electra said.

'Oh.' Gran looked lost for words. The sea mouse swam on to her hand and nuzzled her with his little fluffy, pointed nose. Gran's eyes filled with happy tears. 'Oh,' she whispered, stroking him. 'He's perfect.'

The mouse squeaked happily.

Gran looked so delighted that Electra felt a warm glow spread through her.

'We're sorry about the mess, Dad,' Sasha said.

'Yes, and we really will tidy everything up,' said Sam.

'Don't be cross with them, Ronan,'

Gran said. 'They were only trying to make me happy. This is the most wonderful birthday surprise I have ever had!'

Ronan looked around helplessly. 'All right. I won't be cross so long as you all help clear up.'

'I'll fetch some cleaning things,' Gran said. She swam into the kitchen with Ronan.

Remembering the mess there,

Electra hastily swam after them. 'It's a bit untidy in here too,' she said apologetically.

Gran stopped with an exclamation as she saw the cake on the table. 'You made me a cake too!'

'It got a bit burnt,' Electra said, looking at the wonky cake – the icing had dripped and the letters had run together. It didn't really look very good. 'And it was going to be bigger.'

'Well, burnt or not, I think it looks wonderful!' Gran said loyally. 'I can't wait to try some!'

Electra remembered the sea snakes'

reactions to the cake. 'I think it might be more of a cake to look at than to eat,' she said, a bit unhappily.

Ronan squeezed her shoulder. 'In which case I think we should get everywhere cleared up and then go out for tea and cake at the mermaid cafe – what do you think, Electra?'

Electra's unhappiness melted away. 'I think that's a brilliant idea!' she said.

With all of them working together, it didn't take long to get the cave back to its normal tidy state. Ronan rehung

the banner and the streamers and
they all helped clear up the paint and
glitter and the mess in the kitchen.
They had just finished when the shell
curtain tinkled and Maris came in.

'Goodness, this place looks tidy!'
she exclaimed.

Electra and the others grinned at
each other.

'We were just going out to tea,'
Ronan said. 'Would you like to come
too, Maris?'

'Yes, please,' replied Maris.

They swam to the cafe and sat down to an amazing tea with sea-cucumber sandwiches, iced biscuits shaped like sea horses, jam tarts in the shape of starfish, and sea-strawberry jellies. Ronan bought a huge cake that was put into the middle of the table. It had three layers. The white icing was scattered with tiny multicoloured sugar stars and at the top there was a beautiful anemone made out of sugar.

They sang 'Happy Birthday' and then Gran cut the cake.

'This is just perfect!' Electra sighed

happily as Gran handed out slices. She took a bite of cake. It was delicious!

'It's been a perfect birthday,' Gran told her. The sea mouse popped his head out of her bag and she fed him a crumb of cake. 'And I love Fluffy.'

'Is that what you've called your sea mouse?' Electra asked.

'Yes,' Gran sighed happily. 'You

know, I never thought I'd ever have another sea mouse.' She squeezed Electra's hands. 'Thank you for showing me I'm not too old for sea mice – or for birthdays.'

'No one should ever be too old for sea mice or for birthdays!' Electra told her.

They smiled at each other.

Maris finished her slice of cake. 'So,

did everyone hear the news about the sea snake?' she asked.

They all shook their heads.

'It's gone. It was seen swimming out to sea away from the reef. Although there wasn't one but two sea snakes – a baby and its mother.'

Gran shivered. 'Thank goodness they didn't get through the reef. The mother could have been really dangerous.'

Maris nodded. 'The mermaids who saw them said that both snakes had a big bulge in their stomachs. They must have eaten something but no one can work out what it was.'

The adults frowned thoughtfully.

'I wonder what it can have been?' Ronan said.

'It's a real mystery,' Maris said.

Electra glanced at Splash. His eyes sparkled. 'More cake, Electra?' he whistled.

She grinned at him. 'Yes, please!' she said.

Do you love magic, unicorns and fairies?

Join the sparkling

Linda Chapman

fan club today!

It's FREE!

You will receive
an exciting **online newsletter** 4 times a year,
packed full of fun, games, news and competitions.

How to join:
visit
lindachapman.co.uk
and enter your details

or send your name, address, date of birth* and email address to:

linda.chapman@puffin.co.uk